THE DARKNESS WITHOUT

ROBERT TILLSLEY

This is a work of fiction. All characters, organisations, locations, and events portrayed in this novel are either products of the author's imagination or are used fictitiously.

Thanks to the following alpha/beta readers: Aaron Holding, Teresa McPherson, Monika Tillsley, Michael Walley.

The Darkness Without

Cover design by Robert Tillsley

All stock images used with permission.

Published by Black Sky Books

Magill, Australia

www.blackskybooks.com

ISBN 9780645388664

A catalogue record for this book is available from the National Library of Australia

BOOKS BY ROBERT TILLSLEY

NOVELS

Project Eclipse

The Last Cruise Ship (as R Max Tillsley)

The Darkness Without (Novella)

SHORT STORIES

Replication — Contact This! (anthology), Crickey! — Storming Area 51 (anthology), Contours of War — On Deadly Ground (anthology), Red Snow — Slay Bells Ring (anthology) , Silent Griffin — Fire For Effect (anthology), Where the Dead Walk — The Monster Within (anthology), Bloodstone — Zombie! Patient Zero (anthology), Clay Breath — Clash of Steel (anthology)

CHILDRENS BOOKS

All as R Max Tillsley

THE SUSIE STEELE ADVENTURES

The Steele Trap

The Steele Bite

TANGLED FATES

Brainz

The Winter King

STAND ALONE NOVELS

Rebyrth

CHAPTER 1
SNATCH

Ever feel that days are flowing down the drain, one pointless bit of drudgery chasing another? That you can't even remember how you got to where you are or where it all went wrong? That was me. They say it takes sacrifices to change your life, only they don't tell you who has to be sacrificed.

A motorcyclist cursed and dodged around me as I crossed the narrow lanes of Oberon Street. I returned the greeting with a finger. He'd had plenty of room. Moments later, trash swirled in the wake of a rusting sedan, only to settle against the flat tire of a long-abandoned Chevy Suburban. I walked alongside an overgrown park surrounded by a chain-link fence, where a heavy padlock kept people out or the plants in. The nearby street lamp blinked, then died for good, leaving dusk to fade into a cloudy night sky.

"Hey, Julian," said a kid from in front of 248, "I kicked my soccer ball into your tree again. Can you get it?"

That was the second time this week. Ben was about ten years old. His blond hair was already over his eyes again—it grew like kudzu, and he was always out front, kicking a ball around the small patch of grass in front of his house. It was a two-story brick construction, squashed up against rows of its neighbors, just like mine on the opposite side.

I'd never met his parents. And I'd never seen him step so much as onto the sidewalk. His only company was an ugly garden gnome with chipped paint that held a little pitchfork. Something wasn't quite right about the kid's home situation, so, I kept an eye on him. And his soccer ball.

I glanced up at the red maple that crowded the front of my house. Among the brilliant red of its autumn leaves nestled a white ball with blue and rose-gold highlights. I pulled my hands out of my well-worn hoodie and leaped up, tapping the ball free.

"Here you go." I waited for the ball's second bounce and kicked it across the street.

A grin stretched across his narrow face. "Thanks, man."

"Just work on your aim."

"You got it."

I walked up the few stairs to my front door, jiggled the key into the troublesome lock, and entered. The TV tried to sell me on a new skincare cream, an overlayed message asking if I was still watching, even as the advert looped with some kind of glitch. The lumpy couch beckoned. My aging laptop sat at one end next to my headphones.

Welcome to my office.

A door opened onto the kitchen-dining combo, and another went through to a bathroom. The narrow staircase on my left led to the upper floor with my bedroom and another room filled with junk from the last tenant—junk that I'd been putting off clearing out since forever. They'd been a real oddball.

I slipped a small bottle of whiskey from my hoodie pocket and collapsed onto the couch. Ancient springs twanged in protest. What a damn day. My water had been disconnected. The company's chatbot kept insisting I still had water, and I'd gotten sick of being on hold for two hours to talk to a real human. Go to their office, I'd thought, stay until someone fixed whatever was up.

They don't do things in person, the receptionist had told me. I'd told her they didn't do shit remotely, either. And at that point, security tossed me outside. Two hours of subway delays each way. Why even bother getting out of bed?

My stomach rumbled, but I took a pull from the whiskey bottle and reached for the TV remote.

A cacophony of beeps assaulted my skull, battering my brain with an unholy glee. I shoved my hands over my ears, dislodging the empty bottle, which landed on a threadbare rug with a thud. Ants had crawled into my mouth, spreading dirt. At least that was the sensation I felt. My dry tongue whipped against my equally dry lips as I searched for the source of multiple alarms.

Light flickered at the edge of the curtain. It was outside. I pushed myself off the couch and went to the door, rubbing my eyes the whole way. When I opened it, my jaw dropped.

Flames leaped from the ruins of number 248. The house had collapsed inward as if a giant fist of fire had punched down on the roof. The buildings on either side were mostly intact, but the flames were already spreading. Little gray feathery flakes drifted down like dirty snow. My already rough throat now felt like I was breathing in flour dust. I coughed and spat. It didn't help. Smoke spread toward the sky, seeking the clouds.

Ben. It was night. The kid would have been in there. Had there been a warning? Had he escaped along with his parents? Car alarms blared their dismay, but where were the sirens, the firefighters, the paramedics, the police? Hell, where were the bystanders, the neighbors filled with morbid curiosity?

I hurried past the maple, my eyes darting up as if expecting the soccer ball to be waiting for my help. There was no traffic, so I crossed the road without pause and stopped on the grass where the kid had stood earlier.

Heat slapped my face over and over. Damn, I needed a drink. My gaze went back and forth across the burning wreckage, and horror settled in my bones. No one could have survived whatever had happened. Maybe a gas explosion. It looked more like a satellite had crashed. The poor kid.

"Where were you?" A small, gritty voice demanded over crackles and pops.

I must have imagined it, the voice of a guilty conscience, I thought, because no one was there.

"Down here."

The garden gnome sat, legs out straight, back resting on the lowest step. One leg, at least. The other had shattered, the fragments sprayed across the grass. The top of his little rake had snapped off, and there was a hole in the once jaunty red cap on his head.

The chubby face glared at me.

I took a step back, wondering if the whiskey had been tainted.

"I couldn't stop them," the gnome hissed through clenched teeth, one hand shakily moving to the hole in his cap. "And you didn't come. They took him, then the dragon wreaked havoc. Why didn't you come?"

I dropped to one knee, inexplicably moved by the gnome's plight, his pleading.

"I—I don't know. I'm sorry. What can I do for you?"

"Nothing. But the boy. The forest gateway will close soon, and the glamor will fade. You have to get the boy."

My brow creased. "Forest?"

He pointed down the street, his ceramic hand wobbling.

"I don't understand. None of this makes sense."

His painted eyes squinted. "The Lion really did a number on you, didn't he? Well, my loyalty was always with you, always. What do you remember?"

"Remember? Of what?"

"Damn. Damn. Damn. No time. Your sword and armor. You'll need them. Hurry. The forest gate." He froze, an ordinary garden gnome once more.

I retreated, coughing, wondering if the smoke had gotten to me. But I glanced down the street where he'd pointed, where the park was, and instead of a fenced-off overgrown mess, I saw a forest. An honest-to-God Sherwood and Robin Hood forest with trees reaching at least five stories tall.

It had to be the smoke. I hurried back to my house, listening for the fire trucks. Why wasn't anyone coming? Standing in my doorway, I checked the park. It was still a forest, a God-damn forest. And some bastard had kidnapped my neighbors' kid. Why was I even considering believing my senses? The answer was simple. It would mean Ben was alive. I wanted it to be true, for there not to be a dead kid, his body crushed and burned under a pile of masonry.

Which was how I found myself running upstairs to the gun safe built into my bedside table. A quick fingerprint scan, and the sturdy door swished open. I collected a compact Glock 19 and a spare mag, then checked a round was chambered. I couldn't remember when I'd bought it, or when I'd last practiced at a firing range, but I fitted an inside-the-waistband holster and secured the weapon with ease. Did I have a concealed carry permit? No, but what people didn't notice couldn't hurt me.

I paused at the top of the stairs, one hand on the door to the spare bedroom. The content had always disturbed me. But now I felt like the idiots in a horror movie who opened a door they didn't need to.

The creak came right out of a B-grade Hollywood production. An assortment of mismatched furniture edged the room, a credenza with chipped faux wood, an imposing wardrobe with carved wooden panels, two nineteen-fifties diner stools, a wine rack with several empty bottles. And on every surface, boxes of worthless trash from old newspapers through to a collection of mismatched spoons.

Weirdest of all was the wagon in the middle of the room. It held rusted armor—not ballistic but the kind you'd see in historical or fantasy shows, down to the helmet, which had a horizontal opening for the eyes and a slit down to the chin, presumably for breathing. A barbute, though I had no idea where I'd picked up the name from. A sheathed sword stuck out, the grip long enough for two hands. If it had been in any better condition, I would have sold it off already.

Your sword and armor. You'll need them.

The garden gnome's words echoed in my mind. I'd take my Glock over this pile of crap any day. But he'd been so sure. Was this something the kidnappers were after? Some old family heirloom? If I could make a trade, it would be worth dragging the stuff along.

Getting a wagon filled with fifty pounds or so of rattling metal down a narrow set of stairs is not easy. I gave up three times, the last when the wagon ran over me. Each time I went to leave without it, I wrestled with indecision, then tried again.

Boy, did I hope that the forest would be gone. I'd know that the fumes had melted my brain. Everything would make sense. But that would mean the kid was dead.

Damn it all.

The wagon clattered onto the street behind me. Ahead, the

forest stubbornly refused to fade away like the mirage it should have been. No sign remained of the chain-link fence. A cool breeze tousled my hair, wafting a sweetness that overcame the oily stink of the city.

I stopped at the abrupt border between cement and dirt. Prints led deeper between the trees. Each had small indents nothing like a modern shoe's tread. There were other marks, too, smaller, deeper holes that could have belonged to several different animals. I swallowed. If I walked forward into an unseen fence, then it would all be over, and a paramedic would be along soon enough to give me oxygen and clear my head.

A dozen steps, and trees surrounded me. *Shit.* I took another ten, watching the ground intently as the wagon bounced along the uneven surface. No doubt about it—I was moving forward. Steeling myself, I spun around, trying to catch reality off guard. It sucker-punched me.

Oberon Street had vanished. Trees continued as far as I could see, some thin-trunked, others behemoths with crowns of blue and gold leaves. It couldn't be real.

Ferns carpeted the forest floor, breaking for distended mushrooms that erupted from the loamy soil. Butterflies zigzagged between drooping bell flowers, and the chitter of unseen insects formed a soundscape as steady as any rush-hour traffic.

"No, no, no," I said, my hand slipping to my Glock.

Yeah, shooting the trees would help. I circled. My footprints abruptly appeared, as with those I was trampling.

"Hello!" The forest swallowed my voice.

Rubbing a sheen of sweat from my forehead, I admitted there was only one option. If that poor kid was here, wherever here was, I needed to stop wasting time and go find him. It wasn't my job, but there sure as hell weren't any cops coming to save the day. What was my job?

I shook my head to clear away an unpleasant mental haze and followed the tracks. The wagon's wheels were wide, the kind suitable for a sandy beach. Here they worked well enough that I accepted the extra effort needed to pull it along. The route veered around large trees, the occasional boulder, and other obstructions. The sun hid behind the thick forest canopy, making it impossible for me to guess where a compass would point. At best, I figured I was continuing in roughly the same direction. Returning would be a simple matter of retracing my steps.

The ground sloped up, and the wagon tugged at my left hand, tiring my arm and shoulder. Only stubbornness made me take it to the crest of a wide hill. The way opened up at its distant base. A swift-flowing river stretched to either side, frothing and slapping at its banks. Thankfully, a bridge stretched the sixty feet of its width, though the structure's tumbledown state was less than reassuring.

My route was clear, as was my purpose. And yet, nothing seemed right. How could this be real, and why was I willing to go along with it? I stood there, wasting time, waiting for an answer that refused to show itself. Eventually, I sighed and started down the hill.

What choice did I have?

CHAPTER 2
TOLL

Pulling the wagon downhill was easy, and the energy of the rushing water drew me forward with a strange mixture of excitement and déjà vu. I stopped at the first flagstone, a reddish material with worn patterns engraved on its flat surface. There were no railings or walls on either side. That combined with its mere three feet of width, meant going for a swim would be very easy. The prints stopped at the end of the dirt. This was where the kidnappers had gone, so this was where I needed to cross.

I stepped onto the bridge. It felt sturdy enough underfoot, and its gentle slope upward proved no challenge for the wagon. The air was thick with moisture thanks to the river churning around the bridge's supports, yet it had an unpleasant odor like stagnant water. My hoodie hung heavier on my shoulders. I'd warmed up with the travel, and this place with its overhead sun beating down felt more like spring than fall. Screw worrying about my concealed weapon. I paused and reached to pull my hoodie off. Two things happened at the same time.

The wagon rolled back down the bridge, its path taking it closer and closer to falling off—a thoroughly predictable mistake. At the other end, a long-armed creature scrambled up over the side of the bridge. It had to be eight feet tall. Its fur was a shaggy mustard, its face monkey-like but red. Long arms reached almost to the ground when it stood with hunched shoulders. Every one of its twelve fingers finished with short, conical claws, red to match its face. Two beady eyes glared at me.

Preposterously, a satchel hung from one shoulder and crossed its chest. I half expected it to pull out a phone. A shadow embraced us, then was gone. A bird flying, I thought, but my gaze remained on this creature until metal jingled, and I glanced at the accelerating wagon. One wheel teetered on the edge.

I sprinted and grabbed the handle. The wagon tipped, and I reached for its side as well. Its momentum jerked me toward the water. I leaned back, seemingly trapped in perfect balance for a long time, then slowly dragged the wagon back onto the bridge, remembering this time to set its wheel lock.

"Are you ready?" the creature asked, its voice not as deep as I expected. It was soft and cultured, almost as if I was listening to a friendly librarian.

"Ready for what?" I asked, my hand slipping to four o'clock on my waist, where my Glock waited.

"To pay the toll." Its weight shifted from foot to foot, as if excited.

Maybe it didn't get many people coming through. It might have signed up for a really shitty franchise. My thoughts retraced their steps.

"Did someone else come this way? A group, I think, holding a child."

"We can talk about that once you have paid the toll. Nothing comes for free."

Everyone was hustling these days. The thing probably had

no right to charge a toll. I pulled out my wallet. There was no point making this into a big deal, especially if I could get the lowdown on the kidnappers.

"How much?"

"An arm will do nicely."

"Ha, ha. Look, I don't have much. How about fifty?" I pulled out a couple of creased twenties and a ten. "I won't even ask for a receipt."

The creature opened its mouth wide and roared, its breath drenching me in a blast of fetid air. "Puny mortal. Who are you to mock a troll?"

Troll? I glared at the bridge, trying not to connect the dots. I put away my wallet and reached for my Glock. The weight steadied my hand as I slipped it free. I brought it into a two-handed grip, trigger finger along the barrel, which pointed directly at the creature.

"I'm Julian, the guy with the gun. And I've played your game, troll. I answered your question. How about you back up and start answering mine? No one needs to get hurt."

The troll advanced, using its knuckles to swing its legs forward in a strange gait. "No, stupid mortal. You will hurt. A lot."

Adrenaline coursed through me, and the pistol shook. I took a breath. There was no time for a warning shot. It had built up speed and would hit me like a bus. I squeezed the trigger.

There was a sad pop, and the bullet dropped out of the barrel, hitting the bridge after a short distance. I'd never seen a dud round do that, but I racked the slide, kicking out the used casing and bringing in a fresh round. I fired again.

Another pop. This time, the bullet didn't even leave the damn barrel. My eyes widened in horror. I had no defense. "God damn it!"

The troll was almost on me. I did the only thing that came to mind. I threw the pistol at it. It spun end over end, then hit the troll squarely between its eyes. A hiss, then smoke. The pistol bounced away, falling into the river. The troll bellowed, either in pain or anger, and crashed into me.

I flew backward, my feet flailing on the flagstones until I tumbled into the wagon.

The troll loomed over me, saliva dripping from its mouth. "I'll start with a shank."

As it reached for my leg, I noticed its short, pointed teeth. I imagined them biting through skin, tearing into flesh, snapping bone. My hand searched my waist before I remembered I'd already lost the pistol. Desperate, I felt among the random bits of armor until found the sword. It was going to be plastic, some stage weapon with a retracting blade. I rolled, falling out of the wagon and almost off the edge of the bridge. The troll grabbed my ankle, grinding my bones together with its powerful grip.

I grunted and yanked the scabbard off the blade. It hit the bridge with a dull thud, perhaps like that of a piece of meat. The sword weighed maybe three pounds, with three narrow fullers down its length. The edge was thin, the tip pointed. Rust and pits covered its surface. Great. If I cut the monster, it would die from tetanus. Eventually.

Thud, thud.

My head smacked the flagstones, blurring my vision. I cried out in pain and used my free hand to protect my skull. The troll lifted me high by my leg, its jaw opening impossibly wide. A tripartite tongue flicked out in anticipation. Holding the sword tight, I swung clumsily, a single-handed strike. The blade slid along its yellow fur without cutting. A butter knife was sharper.

"Peel off the skin," the troll sang to itself. "There's good stuff within."

It scraped its claws down my leg, catching on my jeans and tearing the fabric along my shin. Lines of agony matched each gash, and red seeped into the blue denim. I struggled, trying to break the troll's grip, but it seemed more amused by my efforts than worried.

"Let the red juice out. Make the meat shout."

So... damn... creepy. My vision swam from the earlier head blows or being upside down or both. I blinked and focused as best I could. With a two-handed grip, I pressed the sword tip against the back of the furry hand locked around my ankle and shoved hard. The blade slipped in a short way, stopping when it hit bone.

The troll released me. "Hey! What do you think you're doing?"

I bent my back as I fell, protecting my head from another battering. This rolled me closer to the troll, where I ended up almost between its legs. I'm not proud, but I'll tell you this: I punched its meaty dong, and when it screamed and grabbed itself, I thrust the sword up through its stomach and into its chest.

It squealed and reeled back, the blade pulling free with a gruesome slurp and spray of pale red blood. My chest heaved as I gasped for air. I scooted away, ready for it to attack. When it fell, I staggered to my feet and approached cautiously.

The troll raised its head, more of the thin blood dripping from the corner of its mouth.

"I thought you a foolish mortal knight, but now I know better. You are *that* Julian, aren't you? I would..." It sagged, then stilled, dead.

"Yeah, okay, so I'm the Julian with the sword. Thanks for not giving me the info I needed, asshole." I looked at my bloody leg. "Fuck. That's great. I'll probably get rabies. And hell, a damn troll under the bridge. I guess that makes me the Big Billy Goat Gruff."

I wiped the blade on the troll's fur. Rust came off with each stroke, leaving shimmering metal too white to be steel. I tested the edge, and now it sliced deeply into the troll's flesh. *It's a good thing*, I told myself even as I cursed its initial bluntness.

A check over the bridge confirmed I'd lost the Glock for good. I threw the spare mag in the water, muttering, and retrieved the scabbard. It had an attached leather belt, so I put it on and slid the sword into place. It would have to do. Or I could just head back, leave the kid, and try to find a way out of the forest. Then I wouldn't need any weapons.

But I'd be a coward. I didn't like that. No one would know, but for some reason, the idea rankled. Onward, it was. I eyed the dead troll in my way.

Damn it. I hated speed bumps.

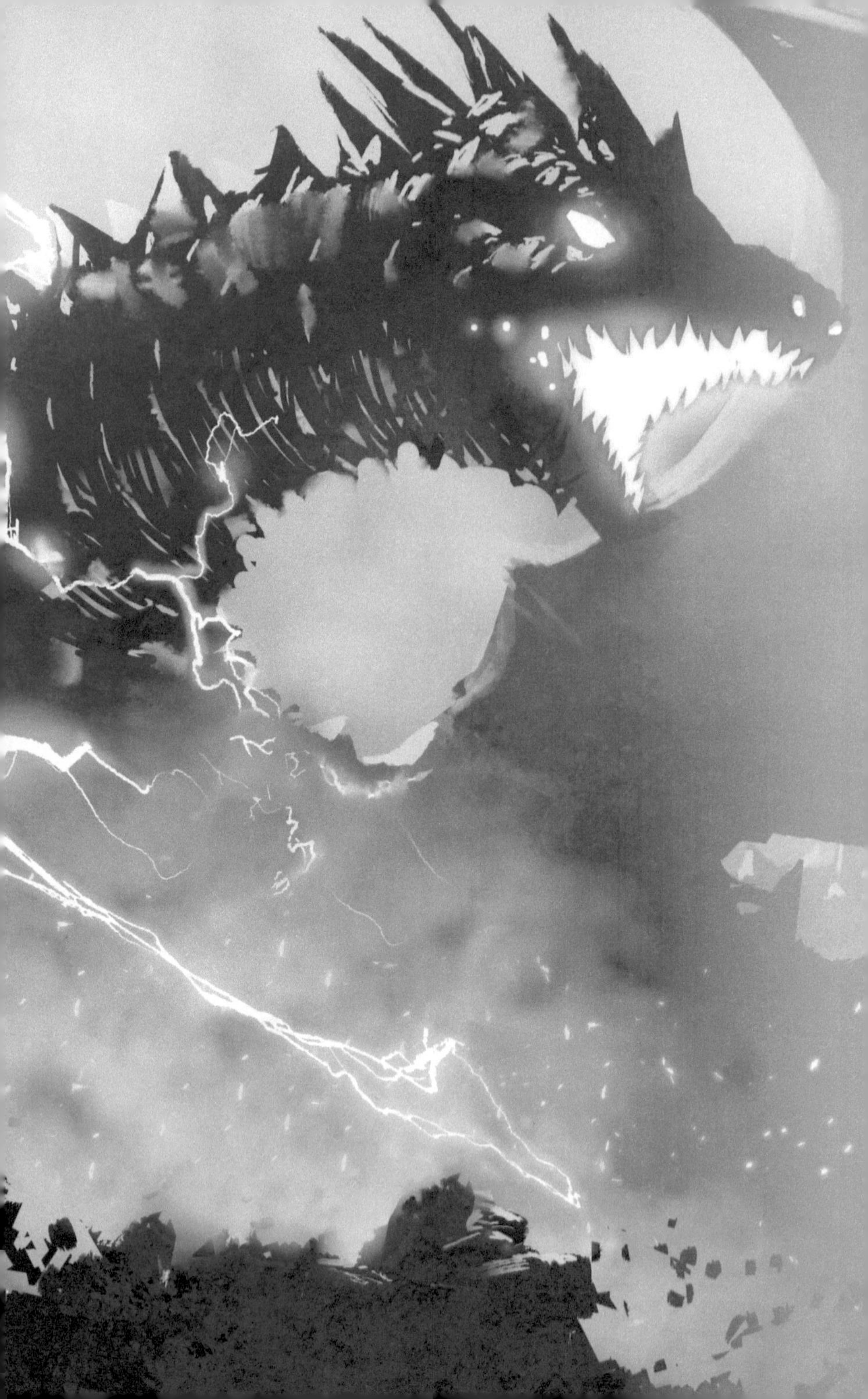

CHAPTER 3
SNARE

I paused to wash my hands in a shallow pool of water near the other side of the bridge. Shoving the troll over the edge to make way for the wagon had been a messy business. Footprints continued to lead me on, though I thought there might be less than before. I returned to the twilight of the forest, leaving the river behind, but on this side, the trunks were less dense, the crowns broader. Fine grass of a brilliant emerald replaced the ferns. They waved gently in all directions, tickled by an unseen wind unable to make up its mind.

My stomach grumbled. I should have brought food. Except that there was no way I could have anticipated walking through an endless forest, and in any city, I would have passed ten or so MacDonalds by now—they were everywhere. How long was this going to take? For all I knew, the kidnappers were pulling ahead, extending the chase with every passing second. Where were they even going?

If they existed at all. If I was walking down a city street, out of my mind on toxic fumes, I'd wander into clean air, eventually. So, shouldn't the hallucinations have faded by now? Unless Ben's parents had been running a drug lab, and I'd breathed in enough crap to melt my brain. If so, the lack of euphoria was a rip-off.

A scratching sound came from off the side of the tracks. I let go of the wagon and put my hand on my sword, eyes searching, ears absorbing every noise. The scratching came again, accompanied by a small grunt, like an annoyed toddler.

I licked my dry lips and walked closer, placing my feet carefully to avoid twigs. I approached the bole of a thick ash tree with teal leaves. On the other side of this, I decided. I drew the sword, wincing at the slight rasp. The ash's bark was rough on the palm of my left hand. I leaned into it while circling the tree.

Fluffy. My brain took several seconds to process the situation. A rabbit with violet and orange stripes like a psychedelic zebra pulled at a snare caught around its rear leg. My first thought was: poor thing. Then my stomach grumbled again. People ate rabbit. I was a people.

The rabbit's head jerked up, its large golden eyes widening.

"Please don't hurt me!" the rabbit cried, cringing as I peered closer.

She wore a small quiver, the arrows spilled across the ground and out of her reach. Further away, a child-sized bow lay, the string snapped.

I didn't want to work out how to cook rabbit anyway. I sheathed my sword and kneeled next to her. "Hold still, and I'll get you out of this."

Her little nose quivered, but she did as I asked, and I worked on a knot.

"It's no good," I said after a little while, shaking my sore fingers, then drawing my sword.

The rabbit erupted into tears. "Oh please, sir. The dragon has killed all the game, and my family is starving. If I die, they shall have no one."

Did the rabbit eat meat? For some reason, that grossed me out. But she'd misunderstood.

"I'm going to cut the rope. Stay still."

She watched the sword intently. I sliced near the knot, and the rope separated, leaving her with an anklet.

As soon as she was free, the rabbit bounded several paces away. She turned, her ears sticking up and rotating slowly. Then she bowed.

"Thank you, sir knight. The snare was enchanted against my kind. Any longer, and I would have had to..." Her voice faded and she shuddered. "Soon, I must return to my family, but I owe you a great boon. My name is Jessica Lightfoot. How may I be of service?"

The rabbit collected her arrows, moving on her rear paws, then on all four, and back again. No doubt, she was a fierce hunter of mice or crickets, but I wasn't looking to form a posse. My brow creased as I looked back to where I'd left the tracks.

I pointed in the direction they headed. "Call me Julian. Can you tell me what I'd find that way?"

She froze, one paw-hand resting on her bow. She mumbled my name several times, then said to me. "Do not even think about *that way*. Such a journey will take you to Tirana and the ruins where the dragon lairs."

They took him, then the dragon wreaked havoc.

That was what the garden gnome had said. A real dragon, or some thug with a pretentious name? Thugs sucked—damn assholes who thought they were better than you, who thought the world belonged to them.

I glared at the way ahead. "I don't have much choice. Can you tell me about this dragon, and did you see anyone walking past? It wouldn't have been long ago."

When the rabbit didn't answer, I turned back to her. She was gone.

"Hey," I shouted. "I thought you owed me."

No answer came. *Great boon, my ass*, I thought.

Still, I had learned something. If I found some ruins, I was on the right track. And a track was what I needed to be on. I traced my way back to the wagon, half expecting the contents to have been stolen and not particularly upset about the prospect. Who was I kidding? Only an idiot would want the junk.

A certain idiot grabbed the handle and walked on.

Without an obvious start, a dirt path formed along the footprints that wended its way between the trees. This harder ground didn't mark as easily, and I found myself checking to either side in case my quarry stepped off. Which was how I spotted a graffitied tree.

SET THE PRINCE FREE!

I squinted at the demand, trying to make sense of why it was there. The yellow paint flaked with age, and the letters looked more brushed than sprayed. There was something familiar about them, as if they'd been written by someone I knew. More trees contained messages as I continued, but the weather or time had rendered each incomprehensible. Who was this prince? It didn't matter. Surely, enough time had passed that the guy was either free or resigned to his fate.

Crushed grass stopped my ruminating. I kneeled and inspected the left side of the path. The dirt was churned, and some of it was darker and sticky. I sniffed. Blood. That couldn't be good. Worse were the tracks. It was getting harder to tell, but at least some of the group had continued along the path. Less foot-like tracks, deeper and oddly placed, led from the site of the battle to deeper into the forest.

Ben could have escaped. He was younger and lighter, so he

might not leave prints. But then why would some continue on? Assuming he was still alive, his kidnappers would keep taking him to their planned destination. I should ignore the tracks. I gritted my teeth. Worry fizzled in my bones, a worry without a basis or a speck of reason.

Promising myself that I'd only take a quick look, I hurried off the path, leaving the wagon behind. It was quiet in this part of the forest. I felt like a cliché, but it really was *too* quiet. Distant bird calls should have plucked a delicate song. Small mammals should have scratched or insects chirped. I wasn't sure how I knew this. I couldn't remember being in a forest before this day. Perhaps it was a genetic thing, the kind of knowledge that stayed once we'd left the trees, knowledge that would remain even if we never saw another.

The wind shifted, and sound came from beyond a thicket, grunting, like two pigs going at it, and a voice crying out in anger or fear or both. I'd take a peek, confirm it wasn't my problem, and head back.

Cautious, I drew my sword and advanced.

"What the hell?" I asked myself.

A small house, a kind of country cottage made of white-painted wood, nestled in a vegetable garden. A huge boar with red bristles, yellowed tusks, and a unicorn horn trampled the plants. Oh, and it was wearing a chain mail shirt despite being on all fours. Could nothing just be an ordinary animal in this place?

The boar spun and dashed toward the cottage's door. It hit with a tremendous *thud*. Wood groaned, and screams came from inside, the different pitches suggesting more than one person, a family. None of them sounded like Ben. This wasn't my problem. And yet, that door wouldn't hold out for long.

"Damn it." I walked among the vegetables as the boar retreated from the cottage, no doubt for a run-up.

The beast stopped, its head cocking to one side in a very human gesture of confusion.

"Who are you?" it grunted, an accusation as much as a question.

"No one you'd know," I said, extending my sword tip, "but I'll make bacon out of you if you don't get lost."

It growled, tensed, then charged, careening toward me like a train and probably with a similar weight. I dodged behind a row of plump tomatoes. The boar shifted its path. I rolled, swinging the sword wildly.

Red juice sprayed everywhere like a B-grade horror movie. The boar dashed past, the sword bouncing off its mail. In seconds, it had bled its momentum and turned to face me once more. I, for once, did the smart thing. I ran to the nearest tree.

"You missed," I taunted.

"I know you," the boar growled. "Come out where I can deliver you justice, vile traitor!"

He charged again. I scrambled up the tree. I didn't have time for this, and I'd known it from the start. But creating trouble for myself was kind of a hobby.

The boar slammed into the tree, shaking it. My grip failed. I grabbed wildly, finding nothing to hold on to, and dropped like a stone, leaves slapping at my face like a bonus *fuck you*. My downward trajectory took me right onto the back of the boar, one leg on each side.

I groaned, my balls aching with a sickening intensity, and dropped the sword.

"Get off!" The boar twisted and shook.

I grabbed the only thing in front of me—the unicorn horn—and barely stopped my throat from being impaled on it. Furious, the boar slammed against the tree, pinning my leg, then leaped to the right and bucked. I held on with terror-fueled strength, and a strangled laugh escaped my lips. This was insane.

The boar sprinted, turned, sprinted again, then jerked its rear to one side. I slid to the right, instinctively putting one hand down to protect my head. My fingers touched the cold metal of my sword. I grabbed for the handle and lost my grip on the boar's unicorn horn, deciding it was a fair trade. Rolling twice, I tasted dirt, then came to my feet, sword in hand.

A yellowed tusk pierced my stomach, and small amber eyes glared, inches from my own. I gasped, thinking of the armor back in the wagon as the boar lifted me off the ground.

"For the regent!" the boar cried.

I grabbed its horn. "Well, this is for me, you triceratops reject." Fighting off nausea and pain, I stabbed into the boar's neck, missing the chain mail and parting muscle in a bloody shower.

It gurgled and collapsed, dislodging me. I tried to step back, but it was like I was issuing commands to a cat. My body refused to acknowledge the attempt.

Wind swirled, and I was looking up at the sky. One side was bruised, a hint of a coming dusk. My clothes were moist. I'd wet myself, or I was bleeding a lot. Most likely, the latter.

Three wolves appeared at the edge of my vision, staring down. They were bipedal and clothed in dresses or tunics and pants from a bygone era, each brightly colored, and with no zips or buttons.

The one in pants put a furry hand on my forehead.

"We should have known you'd come. I should never have doubted you. Please, forgive me."

Another in a dress snapped sharp teeth, then said in a motherly voice. "We waste time and his precious blood. Help me carry him."

They grabbed me by my shoulders and feet. Excruciating pain burned through my nerves. I struggled, driven by an instinctive fear. They were going to eat me. And Ben was on his own. It was my fault. Everything was my fault.

Blessed darkness washed it all away.

CHAPTER 4
BLEED

A sickly-sweet cinnamon scent with a touch of something earthy tickled my nose. My mouth tasted of blood. Feet scuffed. Glass clinked on wood. Whispers danced across an unseen room, giving me the sense of a large but not huge room, one filled with enough things to mute echoes.

I opened my eyes. At the far side, a stone hearth held a bubbling cauldron. Four rickety chairs had been pushed to one side. A rough woven mat held a small wolf in a patched white nightdress playing with simple wooden dolls. Shelving held a butter churn, pottery, brushes, and tools. Herbs dangled from rafters, along with cooking utensils. A spinning wheel had a small stool pressed against it. Sacks of grain almost buried two long chests. Whitewash brightened the walls, punctuated by twin unglazed windows currently blocked by heavy shutters.

A single lantern rested on a hook above a long waist-high bench, adding to the light of the fire, the pair giving the room a soft, intimate glow. A wolf—the mother, I guessed—cut something unseen with steady chops of her knife.

There was a click, the padding of feet, and the male wolf

entered from a door to the rear of the room. He held a bucket that sloshed as he favored his left leg. Each of the three wolves had white cloth wrapped around one arm, thick enough to create a slight bulge.

"There, enough water for the night." He placed it carefully on one end of the bench and turned to the young wolf. "Betsy, you should be asleep."

"But I don't want to miss *him* waking."

"I'm awake," I said, my voice thin with trepidation.

The mother turned. "I told you we should have carried him to the bedroom."

"He was losing too much blood, and if my knee gave way..."

I put my elbows beneath me and tried to sit up.

"Please, wait, your majesty." The mother wolf scooped up a small clay flask and hurried to me. "You haven't drunk the second dose. Your wound will not have knitted together yet."

My stomach felt like that damn boar's tusk had been stuck in again, so I dropped to my back, sweat hot on my brow. "Yep. I can believe that. Where am I?"

"In our home," the father wolf said as he hovered over his wife's shoulder. "It is simple, but we have always supported you, and anything of ours is yours."

"Ah, thanks."

The mother wolf leaned closer, her teeth glistening. "You need to drink all of this up, every last drop."

I reached for the flask, my shaking hand unable to hold its weight.

"Let me, if you will." She brought the flask to my lips and poured some in.

I swallowed, then tried to move my mouth away, gagging on the coppery aftertaste. I thought of a hot cross bun dipped in blood.

Her lips pulled back, terrifying me. "I beg of you, do not

resist. The potion is as strong as I could brew it in the time we have, but it is still weaker than I trust. Every drop matters."

The truth was that I was completely helpless. If they wanted to kill me or force this goop down my throat, they could do it. I sighed and decided to be a good patient. It still tasted awful.

"There, all done. May I check the wound?"

"Sure, yes, thanks." At least it put off the potential for a third dose.

I lay on several blankets, a short distance off the ground. She pulled back a thin blanket that covered me, stopping just above my groin. My hoodie and shirt were gone. I wiggled, confirming I still wore my pants, which was oddly reassuring. A red patch of skin the size of a half-dollar sank a short way into the left side of my bare stomach. A spiderweb of darkness surrounded it.

The wolf leaned close and sniffed. "Yes, better, I think."

Her tongue shot out from between her sharp teeth and she licked the wound, teaching me what vulnerability really was. I gulped but kept still.

"Yes, the poison fails. You will recover, though you should sleep until dawn."

I closed my eyes. How much time had I already lost? "I can't. I need to go. Someone's counting on me."

"We're all counting on you," the father wolf said with reverence, as I swung my feet over the side.

They both retreated a short way and lowered themselves to one knee. "Betsy," hissed the mother, and the young wolf joined them, her eyes wide and curious even as her parents bowed their heads.

"Don't do that. Stand, please. I'm not who you think I am. I'm just a guy going to help someone."

The father wolf chuckled. "May I share our names?"

"Of course. I'm Julian."

He nodded as if he'd already read my driver's license. "I am George. I used to be a foot soldier in the resistance."

"And you still think you are," growled his wife. "I am Asena, herbalist for all and healer to this old fool. Our daughter is Betsy."

"Aye," George said, almost meeting my gaze. "She has the right of it. Fool, I am. I was searching for mushrooms when I saw Arthus. I had my crossbow, and I couldn't pass up the chance to take out the regent—may his mane grow sticky with his own blood. In my haste, I missed his retinue, and my crossbow bolt missed him. When I ran—"

"Your knee gave way, and you brought that boar back home," Asena stated. "Fool."

"Yes, well," George hung his head. "I make amends as I can. Lord Julian, I have brought your armor. I swear I oiled and polished it, but I cannot shift the stains. It rusts like iron. You had no arming doublet, so I took the liberty of adjusting mine."

"You took—" Asena started.

"We took," George corrected. "Lord Julian, you are not so different in size to when I fought. It would be my honor if you wear it."

I hesitated, and Asena snapped at the air. "Even tainted armor can turn aside a sword or a tusk."

"Thank you. I will, but I really have to go." I struggled to my feet, aware of the pain and surprised at how manageable it was. The wolf knew what she was doing. But I didn't relish the weight they wanted to hang off me.

George bowed, went to a corner, and returned with folded clothing. This was how it was going to be, I realized. No point fighting it.

The arming doublet fit though George had added a strip of canvas down the back to give my shoulders more room. It was a strange garment with many leather cords hanging here and there. The front was closed via a cord that had to be wound through holes in an upward spiral, a gap making me look like a stripper. My jeans had also been repaired with large stitches that reminded me of Frankenstein's monster despite their neatness. I wasn't going to win any fashion awards.

Asena wandered away, issuing commands to Betsy, who kept glancing at me. George retrieved the armor piece by piece, hanging it off cords and buckling straps. The weight wasn't as bad as I feared, and it all fit me remarkably well, right down to the legs that enclosed my limbs like a tin can. I didn't want to think about what I'd do if nature called.

As George worked, I noticed red seeping through the white fabric around his arm.

"You're bleeding. Did the boar hurt you?"

Asena's ears twitched. "No, but every magic needs its sacrifice."

Magic? The only magic I'd seen was the potion. My gorge rose. It had tasted like blood because it had been blood. They all had the bandages. They'd bled themselves for me—right down to the kid. I felt awful.

"That was very generous. Thank you. I owe you."

"You saved our lives," George said as he adjusted a strap. "And our oaths remain unbroken. If there was a debt, it was ours to repay. I would go with you if you would have me, but my knee would only slow you down."

"The boat," Asena said, filled a leather backpack.

George stood. "I was getting to that. Lord Julian, we have a small boat by the shore of Boine River. It would take you swiftly to Tirana if that is your destination."

A boat trip in armor. *Oh, goodie.*

CHAPTER 5

PROMISE

There were a thousand questions I should have asked, not the least being how to steer a boat. But the big ones pressed on me. What was this world? Who exactly was I chasing? What was this city I headed toward? Who did they think I was? And one that I really couldn't believe I hadn't considered earlier—why had Ben been kidnapped?

However, driven by a strange desire not to let down this family of wolves, this pack, I had put on a mask of nonchalance and climbed into the wobbling bucket of wood beside a small jetty. It stunk of rot. Asena had leaned over and lit a lantern at the prow of the boat, and George had pushed me into the current with well-wishes and not a little desperation. He expected something from me. They all did. Well, the youngest wolf, Betsy, just waved like I was a passing movie star.

The water didn't care for me nearly as much. The boat soon bucked and rocked, threatening to toss me overboard. While trying to steady myself, I kicked my helmet, and it went straight into the water. It was not my proudest moment, and if Betsy could still hear me, she'd have learned a few new phrases. The lantern glow barely reached thirty feet, allowing me just enough time to contemplate my screw-up before I spotted my impending doom. I dodged a fallen tree, and the next one slapped me down, wetting the back of my head. Either spray was getting over the side, or the boat was leaking.

Why hadn't I stuck to the path? I hadn't even asked how far I needed to travel down the river. Above, three moons glowed, the largest taking up almost a quarter of the night sky. Its surface was pocked, creating the illusion of movement. And then an eye opened on it, a big round eye with a pale gray iris and a pupil with an oily sheen. It stared down, so massive that I must have been invisible, and yet, I felt as if it were examining me. I sat up, disliking the impression, and found a box which I dragged to the middle of the boat to sit on. There were also two oars. I wasn't at the mercy of the current and sitting was a lot more stable than standing.

After placing the oars in their rests, I tested the ends in the water, finding the pressure as telling as if they were extensions of my body. Never before had I been in a boat, not that I could remember. My youth was a haze of happiness, sadness, and anger—the details locked away, leaking only sensations.

A large rock jutted out of the water, and my muscles knew what to do, guiding the oars that in turn charted a safe route closer to the center of the river, which was only a little more than sixty feet across. Trees haunted the murky banks, huge fireflies burning in their branches like radioactive fruit.

Now I had the boat under control, it wasn't taking on any more water. I rowed with the current, caught up in a moment of calm, repetitive effort until I spotted a partially submerged wreck. Shifting the boat around, I let it continue tail first. Ropes held a sail to a shattered mast, the cloth whipping back and forth in the water. This was recent. I stared downriver. A pulsating red glow tinged the horizon, unlike any dawn on

Earth. I breathed in deeply and caught the scent of smoke, its dry taste acid on my tongue. That couldn't be good.

With little choice, I continued, standing with steady feet and shifting my balance with ease as I passed a second sunken ship, then a third.

The river widened quickly, the current slowing as it fed into a great lake, the trees on the bank giving way to a city.

"Tirana." The word came to my lips unbidden.

The docks should have been filled with ships, a maze of wood that sucked in goods like a pair of lungs. Instead, a great expanse of the lake's shore was a graveyard of blackened stumps that cradled nothing but death. Behind the skeleton of the docks, the remains of warehouses coughed up smoke, hiding the city. The red glow told me all I needed to know—it, too, burned.

I took up the oars once more and rowed steadily to where the smoke was thinnest, coming alongside a charred ladder by a stone wall, which I climbed.

Devastation met me, and I walked with it. Behind the warehouses huddled rows of two-story buildings with blackened or missing roofs. Bodies littered the streets, many wearing clothes of linen or leather. None were human. A badger lay, one arm out next to a bag of spilled gold coins. Five otters huddled against a small wagon, never to move again. Despite inspecting them closely, I saw no signs of injury. That changed as I crested a small rise.

The buildings curved down, giving me a view across the city. At the far end, a single, steep hill dominated, its top flattened and covered with ruins, the details lost to distance.

Closer were the remains of a battle, perhaps thirty or forty bipedal bodies. One side wore chain mail with a yellow tabard with a stylized sun that was distorted into an oval. They were sheep, black, white, or brown. Some had crushed skulls, others bloody wounds where chain links had failed. The sheep soldiers had once carried short, curved swords and shields. Their likely opponents were a mix, both in type and dress. A beheaded sloth still held a spiked mace in its long claws, while three bushy-tailed squirrel corpses in thick leather sleeveless jackets splayed their limbs near miniature spears. A cougar in a baggy shirt had collapsed atop a sheep, her rapier running through its neck, the snapped tip glued to cobblestones with viscous blood.

Who had won? Maybe they'd all lost. My gaze swept across the city once more. What was one kid's life against this slaughter?

"It's the life I can save," I told myself.

That was damn arrogant. The truth hit me hard. I'd made a mistake. The boat had taken me swiftly to the city, but I'd lost track of the kidnappers. The wolves had assumed I wanted to get to Tirana, and... so had I. It felt right. It still did. And yet...if the lion had come here, assuming that was their goal, Ben could already be dead, or the fires could be threatening him right now. My head buzzed with questions, with indecipherable strands of noisy thoughts. I needed information, not recriminations.

I circled the dead and moved on, hurrying lest despair run me down. A distant roar or explosion—it sounded a little like both—shook me. Slate shingles rattled off an official-looking building, raining down on the street, shards *plinking* against my armor.

Taking a right turn when blocked by a barricade, I moved down a narrow lane, wishing I'd thought to bring the boat's lantern with me. When it opened into a garden of some kind, I gave thanks. Then I smelled death.

More bodies, this time a mixture of civilians and combatants, as far as I could tell. Many of the former had their innards ripped out, and the stench of offal soured my stomach. Looking up, I searched for calm. The moons had shifted, along with the stars. Dawn was coming, not right away, but it was on the march. That meant something. My brow furrowed.

"If you've come to finish me off, you would only be doing me a favor." The voice was bizarre, a mournful high-pitched vibration.

I drew my sword and approached. A duck as tall as my hips lay by a pond, a trail of blood showing how it had dragged itself close. One wing rested in the dirty water. Sharp spurs strapped to its webbed feet were stained, showing their purpose. A thick-shafted crossbow bolt stuck out of the creature's chest.

"Don't fear me," I said to the duck as I kneeled, my eyes scanning for trouble. "Can you tell me what happened?"

"Tell you? Do your eyes fail you? Have your ears been covered all these moons?"

"Something like that."

The duck quacked mournfully, then said, "We'd had enough. The dragon kept coming and coming and coming. We stopped believing the regent's excuses. And those of us who'd been part of the resistance remembered who we were. He'd said he'd personally lead the way up to its lair when the time was right, but he didn't. He built his watch towers with their ballistae, keeping his city safe even as the beast nested in plain sight. We died tending our crops and our crafts—all the people of Alfhimar—while he sat and played king under *its* very shadow."

Dragon. The word resonated in my mind and weakened my limbs. He meant a real dragon. A fire-breathing one.

I gestured to the horrors around us. "And all this?"

"He has something to kill the dragon. He's had it from the start. Everyone knew it. We protested, demanding he use it. When that failed, we attacked to slay him and do it ourselves. And now it doesn't matter. We're all dead. My brothers. Five of us there were. I'm the last." His body shook, and his feathers ruffled.

I thought of the rabbit and the wolves. "There are still *people* out there. And speaking of that, there's someone I'm looking for, a child." I thought of all the animals. Were there any humans in this world? Could these creatures tell the difference between us? "He looks a bit like me. There's a lion who kidnapped him." I gestured vaguely upriver. "He would have come that way on foot."

"Lion?" The duck blinked, its bill opening slightly. "The regent kidnapped—" It sucked in air and tilted its head. "It's you, isn't it? You've come back. Thank the stars. I saw you once when I was a duckling. This changes everything. The battle was worth it if we cleared the way. You are going to save Prince Benedict?" The question was genuine as if the answer could go either way.

Prince? Why not? If the kid was from this crazy land, it actually made a twisted kind of sense. I'd stepped into a game of deadly politics. But why did the duck recognize me? Perhaps from a photo of Ben's?

I gingerly placed a hand on the bird's soft neck. "I will save him. Do you know where they took him?"

"It started with the dragon. The law of duality requires it to end there. My prince."

The duck slumped. Its chest stilled.

So, the regent was after the prince, and it had something to do with the dragon. I thought back to what the wolves had said about magic. It required a sacrifice.

Oh, shit. The regent was going to sacrifice Ben to the dragon, to appease it or something. It was a princess in the tales I'd heard, but clearly, a prince would do. And if he was going to do that, then he'd need to reach the dragon. And where would a dragon have its lair? The duck had said the regent had been living under its shadow. If that was literal...

I stared through the smokey haze at the hill with its ruins. That had to be it.

"I'm going to save him," I told the dead duck.

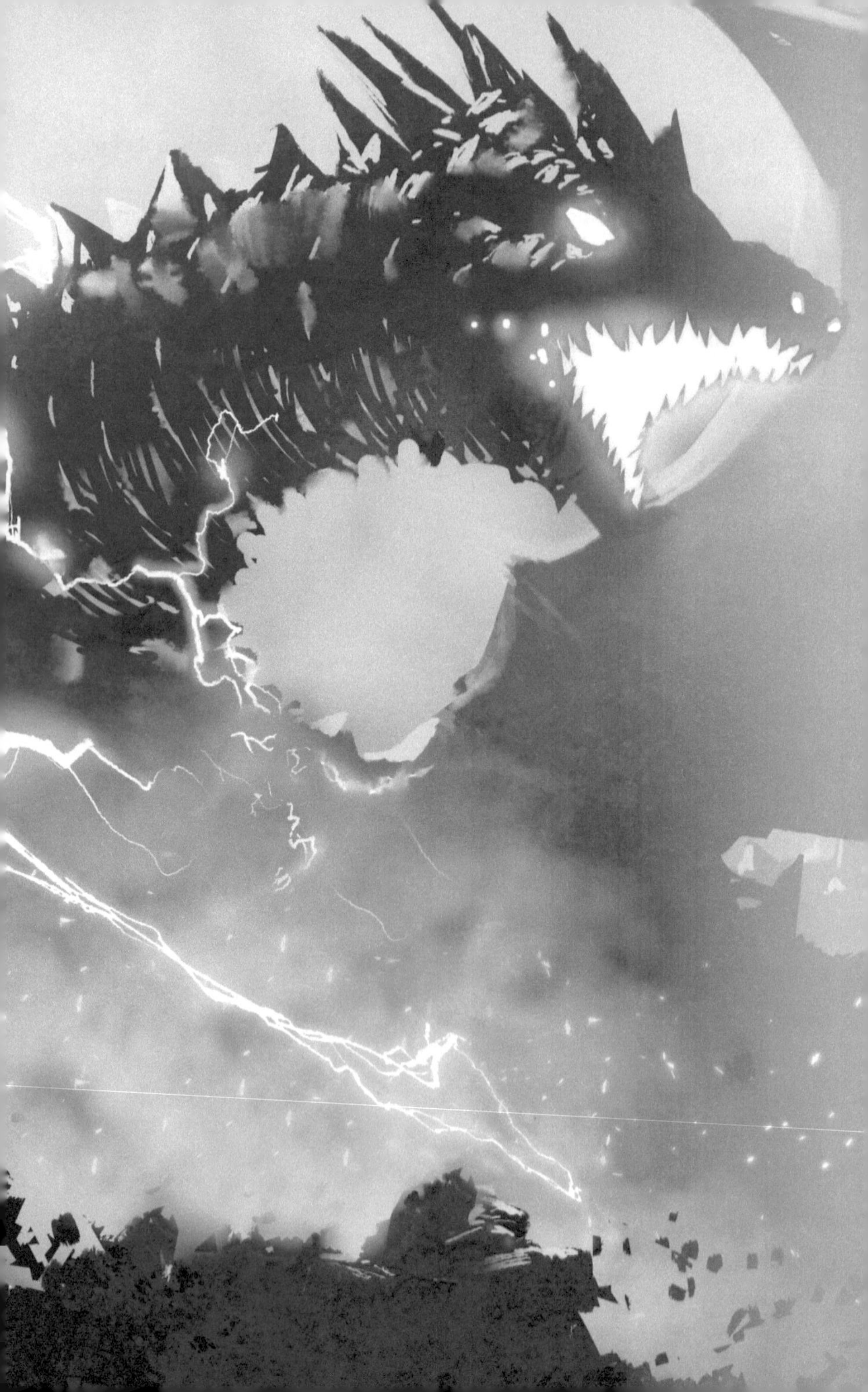

CHAPTER 6

OUTFOX

Heat from a burning stable seared my left side. My skin prickled beneath the armor, and my breath rasped. I pressed on, having picked this route for its directness, not its comfort. Streets twisted this way and that, yet I felt confident that I hadn't been turned around. Sure enough, once I cleared a crumbled wall, I saw that I had reached the end of the city.

Before me, a winding path of neat stone flags led up the hill. Red maples lined it on both sides, and there was no sign of the debris that clogged the streets I'd traveled. The moons had all set, and the sky was navy and gray and crimson. Light from the terrible fires played on the trees. I snorted. There was something almost tranquil about the setting, a peace entirely out of place. I thought of Hansel and Gretel, and the house made of sweets. Well, it was time to bite.

I marched forward and up. The armor was surprisingly quiet, the joints flexing smoothly with my movements rather than clattering like deranged bells. And the weight, while noticeable, didn't exhaust me as I had expected. For once, things were going well. And then I turned at the second switchback.

Two foxes sat, one on a wooden box, the other on an overturned wagon. Their fur was a rich burgundy, and they wore tight-fitting black outfits like in old ninja films. Both held swords across their laps, the weapons similar to my own, if plainer.

"Lord Julian," said one, standing. Her voice was smooth like honey. "The Lord Regent thought you might show."

"Arthus is a canny master," the second added. His voice had a whiny tone.

I nodded as if I knew this to be true. Arthus was the lion, and these were his minions. That much was clear. Which meant this could only end one way, one good way. First, I needed information.

"It has been a while," I said, hoping they'd take the bait and give it meaning.

"Thirty summers," the vixen agreed. "You have grown weak."

"It's all the pizza. I can't say no to a double pepperoni—I'm only human, right?" I was stalling, seeking a way to tease more from her. My humor wasn't going to do it. Did she know me personally? It was worth testing. "Look, obviously things have gotten a little strained between us—"

She gripped her sword tightly, the tension clear despite her fur. "Strained? You slayed the king and queen. You set the dragon upon us. Thirty cycles of misery have beset our people, and now the Lord Regent must do that which will break his heart to bring it to an end. I *never* knew you."

Her accusation hit me as sharply as her sword could have. She did know me. An image of a medieval pub filled with animals and other blurred forms impossible to make out. Tankards in our hands. I knew her. I knew this place, this city. I had ascended this hill. The ruins were once a castle. The certainty came tumbling over me, an avalanche of revelations threatening to bury me.

"Ha," she said, reading something in my strained expression. "I did not think you capable of shame."

"He deceives, sister," the male fox said, also standing.

"I have his measure."

Was she right? I couldn't say. When I tried to weave more threads of memory together, they slipped out of my grasp.

I shook my head to clear my mind. They could be playing me. She might be using magic. I needed to move on. "Look, I don't want to fight you, but I need to pass. I am going to save Ben—Prince Benedict. Screw the dragon, and screw this Arthus."

"Save the prince," the brother mocked. "Save the prince."

The sister raised her sword, leaning the blade over her shoulder. "Attempting to trick a fox is foolish. But to lie so brazenly is insulting. Let us be at it. I have your measure. You may have been mighty once, but now you are nothing but a dirty human."

In an instant, she gripped her sword with both hands and swung at me. I was too flat-footed to dodge back, and my weapon was still in its scabbard. Instinct drove my hand to my sword. Yanking it upward, I threw myself to the right. The blades clanged, but my awkward position gave her an advantage, and she powered through to hit my upper arm. My armor took the blow, and I doubted there'd be so much as a bruise. Maintaining my momentum, I took several steps to gain distance between, keeping my hand high and my sword pointed down in a protective diagonal.

"We don't have to do this," I said.

"But we want to." The brother leaped at a nearby tree, bouncing off its trunk and launching toward me.

"Holy shit!" I shouted, turning to face this new threat.

He swung his sword from high to low. I raised mine, catching his attack on my cross guard. I twisted my wrists, trying to cut around his blade, but he crashed into me, and we both rolled several feet down the path. My head slammed on the stone and scraped off a layer of skin near my temple, the stinging a reminder that I'd been an idiot to lose my helmet.

I punched, but the fox pulled his head back and slipped away, coming to his feet well before I managed the same. The sister observed me intently. She hadn't attacked when her brother had. It might have been an honor thing.

The brother advanced, but the sister pushed him aside, then went at me with a series of blows, one side, then the next, high, low, high. Definitely not an honor thing. She'd been sizing me up. Each time, I parried her attacks, my confidence growing as I found a rhythm to her movement. Which, it turned out, was exactly what she was after.

Halfway through the same sequence, she stopped a strike, pulled back her blade, then cut around the other side of my sword with a small, quick action that sliced my right cheek.

A strange numbness entwined the searing pain. Shock packed my head with cotton wool, and my stomach tried to drag itself free of my body.

"Mine!" the brother demanded, getting in the way of his sister's follow-up thrust to my neck.

She snapped at him with her teeth. He dodged and snapped back, finding only air. But he had moved between us. They were brother and sister, but they were not working together. I shoved him, and he pushed against his sister for balance. Using the distraction, I cut down left to right and severed his head. It rolled off the path, then tumbled down the hill, tongue lolling. The body collapsed, spurting blood like a torn-off fire hydrant. My body trembled with adrenaline, quashing the horror of my deed.

"I told you we didn't have to do this. But I'm going to save the boy."

"Then all would be lost, murderer."

She charged, striking at me with all her strength over and over. I parried as best as I could, trying to maintain some distance so I could move freely. I didn't want to kill her as I hadn't wanted to kill her brother. And it disturbed me that I was ready to do so. At any point before the fight, I could have walked away. The vixen had struck first, but I'd started the fight.

She hit me over and over, slipping between my guard or just blasting through. My armor clanged like a muffled bell, taking the brunt of the blows, but I was collecting bruises. I'd feel some of them for weeks if I lived long enough. And that thought took me off the defensive. Time mattered. We'd both made our choices. I decided to play her game, with a twist.

I struck to her left, pulling the blow and shifting as if to cut around to her right as she'd done to me. But I halted that, too, and instead dropped my tip on the original side and thrust to her chest. She'd been ready to catch the second strike, moving her sword offline, giving my sword a clear path, and I used it to pierce fabric, then flesh, driving in a good foot.

Her blade struck my head, but only with the flat, a dizzying but otherwise harmless blow. We stared at each other as I yanked my sword free.

"Have you not rained enough terror upon our land?" she hissed, blood bubbling out of her mouth.

She collapsed against me, and I held her as her strength failed. Her blood smeared on my breastplate as she grew limp, and I settled her body on the ground.

"Why didn't you let me pass? Why protect a kidnapper, even if it's some Lord Motherfucking Regent? I mean, sacrificing a kid is wrong any way you look at it. If he'd do that, what wouldn't he do?"

No answer came. I cleaned my sword on her clothes and stood, ready to continue. The gore on my armor soaked in like skin cream. The rust faded to nothing, and the metal took on a rich blue luster.

This was how it was meant to be.

Golden feathers sprouted from its shoulders and rolled down to form an ankle-length cape. The whole look was garish, but it came with a familiarity, a rightness. And when I continued up the hill, the feathers shifted, keeping out of my way. I liked it.

I liked it a lot.

CHAPTER 7
BETRAY

Twin oak doors stretched before me, blasted out from the inside, or at least, that was how it appeared. Rubble from the collapsed gatehouse was strewn like blocks of Lego. Among it all, more bodies, more creatures crushed or dismembered. No stench of death remained. Flesh and fur and feathers had given way to bone or dried in a natural display of crude taxidermy. A long time had passed. The carnage sparked anger within me, though I couldn't say if it burned for the waste of life or a deeper, more personal fuel.

I followed a cleared path, imagining the structure and how it once was. My sneakers had changed at some point, hardened, and now rapped the cracked stone floor despite my soft steps. The rear of the gatehouse opened onto a gently upward-sloping expanse of tall grass tangled with large dirty feathers like trash after a concert. Crumbled walls led off to either side, and ahead, the castle waited, as decapitated as the brother fox. It had reached five levels high once, and had seven towers, though only one stood toward the rear. Pinks of an approaching dawn mixed with the red of the city's fire to bathe the white stone with a soft blush that should have been welcoming. To my eyes, it resembled undercooked chicken.

One of the castle's heavy doors was open enough to slip through. I touched the wood, its texture reassuring. *It had not failed.* Failed what? I entered, a growing sense of dislocation clouding my mind. I knew where the doorways would be, where collapsed walls had stood, where stairs waited. Unerringly, I chose a route that avoided dead ends and led me past rotting tapestries and shattered furniture, all the way to the base of the standing tower. There were more feathers, too. It must have been one hell of a pillow fight.

A shadow passed over the broken ceiling above, tugging me like the river's current, a sensation of darkness far greater than the lack of light. To steady my nerves, I drew my sword and started up the tower steps. They were broader than those in medieval movies but circled in the same way. Small slits provided a growing amount of light, each leaving me with a slow strobe effect that added a translucency to the tower's stones. I hurried up the steps, faster and faster, yet an invisible wind pushed against me, or the tower grew endlessly, a beanstalk with a giant waiting above.

Grimacing, I persisted, screaming, "I will not give up. You will not have the kid."

The wind grew almost solid. I pushed with both my mind and my body. Glamor, I told myself, an illusion that created a truth. Screw that. I was going to reach the top. I growled and willed myself forward, inch by inch. The pressure became unbearable. My ears popped. My skin stretched as if it were being ripped off by a giant. I kept trying.

My ears popped. A sensation of snapping followed, then the resistance disappeared, and the tower settled, becoming more real, more solid. I gasped and stumbled but dared not stop here. A dozen steps ahead, an arched doorway waited as if it had always been close. Chunks gouged from one side spoke of the missing door. Grit crumbled under my left hand as I paused to steady myself.

This was it.

Originally, a crenelated wall surrounded the top of the tower, the thick stone providing cover from arrows and wind alike. Sections had been smashed inward, leaving the floor's forty feet of diameter a mess like a scene from a war movie or a paintball field. And feathers, the damn things were everywhere. I glanced beyond, surprised that I didn't fear the height. The distant horizon was pregnant with the oncoming sun, true dawn's birth imminent.

Arthus, Lord Regent of Alfhimar, stood by a slab of stone that had fallen sideways, creating a table or an altar. His great shaggy orange and gray mane spread across his shoulders and disappeared down a breastplate decorated with musculature. He wore an open-fronted cassock of purple with golden edging, the garment kept in place by a belt of woven silver feathers. His hands were furred, the fingers strong, and clawed. He held a wavey-bladed dagger of the same metal as my sword. At one end of the stone, a crown waited, all velvet, gold, and gems intricately aligned to hint at feathers without ever forming the shapes.

I could see child-sized boots at the other end, but his bulk and my distance hid the rest.

Above, a dragon circled. Dirty-gold feathers covered its body and wings like a bird, but it had four legs, a long neck, a ridged head with charcoal scales, a snout, and a gaping mouth filled with twin rows of golden teeth. I gasped, my mouth dry, my heart beating like a drum. Vertigo swatted me, tugging me to the tower's edge, toward the dragon, a crazy desire to jump, to be eaten.

Raising my left arm as a shield, I looked away, my chest heaving. This was the creature that had terrorized the land. Arthus, too, gazed at the terrifying beast. He was mumbling—no —intoning. His deep voice had a presence beyond words, and the rays of sunrise were streaming in toward him. Power gathered, air pressure rising before an oncoming storm that had nothing to do with the weather. He raised his dagger, and it split the growing sunlight like a rainbow, a twisted version of Pink Floyd's Dark Side of the Moon.

"Stop!"

The lion roared.

"Stop?" Fury reverberated through the word. "Stop? Julian, when have *you* ever shown restraint? I cut away your dark half, and still, you are here, refusing to pay your penance."

The dragon swooped low enough for a beat of its wings to swirl dust and feathers. The charged atmosphere held them aloft, hiding the tower floor like a smoke machine, lending a new sense of unreality even in this fantasy world. The dragon's closeness worked its power on me, a waiting drink when I'd had too many, a kick readied when an enemy fell, a word sharper than any sword, a certainty that blinded, an ego that refused all caution, a hunger for revenge, a need to claim my rightful place.

Sapphire blue flames erupted from the dragon's maw, cutting through the air, and dispersing in a mass of coiling, cracking energy. The message it sent was for me, a recognition of our trauma, our separation, an offer of what could be, of what should be. We were one and the same. The dragon completed me.

My sword hovered near Arthus. I'd closed on him while overwhelmed by the dragon. My action hadn't been a conscious choice. That was worrying, I thought as I edged around his bulk, holding him at bay while seeking a glimpse of Ben.

There the boy was, legs and wrists bound with silver cord, mouth covered with cloth tape, an anachronism in this world of magic. His large green eyes stared into my own. Pointed ears stuck up between strands of hair, and I raised my left hand, feeling a definite, if less prominent, point on my own. We'd never been this close before. Our proximity had torn a veil, dispelled a glamor. We were seeing each other as we really were. His features were similar to my own, though younger. My mouth worked as I contemplated a truth that tangled my tongue.

We were cousins. He was an elf. No wonder he looked so young. And I was a half-elf. He was Prince Benedict, heir to the throne. I scowled at the gaps in my mind. Who was I?

"Look upon what you have wrought," Arthus commanded. Disgust burned in his eyes, that and something more I couldn't fathom.

"What I've wrought?" I echoed while wondering whether it was safe to untie the prince. "You kidnapped him, and now you want to cut him up. I'm not the murderer."

He leaned his huge head back and laughed. "Your guile knows no bounds. Do not try it on me, slayer of royalty, kin slayer. Our realm persisted in peace for thousands of years until your taint."

I glanced at Ben. He was small, vulnerable, and his eyes were wide, his body shaking. He hadn't known, but he believed Arthus. And so did I. I'd murdered his parents. An image blasted into my mind like a bolt of lightning. My sword bloodied, dangling from my hand. The king and queen splayed across a white marble floor, crimson pools spreading around them like auras.

A huge paw knocked my blade aside, forcing me into the

present. Arthus leaped upon me, his jaw wide and ringed with perfect, razor-sharp teeth. My eyes widened, but I was already moving. I brought my knees tight to my chest as I slammed down heavily on my back. Claws raked toward my eyes. I kicked out, my legs burning as I sent his heavy form flying over my head and away.

Arthus was a threat to me, but to Ben, he'd be an executioner. I scrambled to where the young prince lay, slipped my sword between his wrists, and sliced the silver cord. It split with a *shiiiick*—sandpaper on concrete.

"Get out of here!" I gestured toward the stairs with my sword. "Hate me if you want, but do it while you're still breathing."

He'd have to untie his own feet. Arthus was already up, and though he'd dropped the dagger, his claws were just as deadly, his teeth deadlier. Rather than attack me, he moved to block the stairs, his eyes darting to the dawn light.

"How did it feel to betray them, to have been accepted as one of their own despite your contaminated blood? To have been the cause of chaos and destruction not seen since the dawn of our kingdom? To have made this child an orphan?"

My memory was still Swiss cheese, but each detail I regained helped me find the edges. It had been torn apart by glamor—elf magic. I'd once been where Ben lay, Arthus glaring down as a dozen armored sheep held me still. Arthus was a druid, a sage within the elven court second only to the king and queen. He'd worked the power of the sun and of the moons, cleaving me in two. As punishment? As revenge?

I wiped my brow, sickened by my actions. I had been greedy. I'd wanted... I couldn't think exactly what. Yet, the result was clear. I wanted something enough to murder. My sword drooped.

"I did it. I remember that now. Hate me if you want. Attack

me. Kill me. But leave the kid out of it. Murdering him won't change what I've done."

"If I could, I would. I tried to excise your darkness for the sake of your mother's memory, but it was too much, your evil too pervasive, and the glamor twisted. Human and dragon, mortal and immortal, the later invulnerable, except by the blood of royalty on the first dawn of the thirtieth year since the deed was done. Not you, though."

The lion laughed cruelly.

"I had a thousand torments to inflict before you died. You have been a thorn in my paw since birth. Yes, your punishment was earned, that and more. I wanted to break you completely, but the resistance smuggled you out of prison. I wonder where they hid you all those years. My soldiers never found so much as a trace. No matter." He grinned, a feral joy. "With the prince's blood sacrifice, I will slay the dragon, and save all, at the cost of the line of elves, a burden I will bear forever. I am willing to pay the price. And if you had any goodness within you, so should you be. Your reign of terror will end, and one of peace will return."

Something told me there was no room in that peace for me. Did I deserve any? I'd murdered two people, Ben's parents. No wonder I'd never seen them across the street or heard them calling him in for dinner.

Holy shit.

The resistance had set me up right next to the kid. Perhaps they believed it was the last place the lion would look for me. I laughed at the balls of it. Arthus had hidden the prince away, never knowing I was right there. But damn, he'd imprisoned the kid as he'd tried to do to me, waiting thirty years for the right time to kill him. There was no other reason for Ben to be tucked away on Earth. After all, he was the next in line for the throne. He should have been in charge by now. Instead, he was stuck playing endless soccer, and I'd been across the road, living a life of small nothings, keeping a friendly eye on him. Both of us glamored. Neither of us aware of what brought us to this point.

I thought of the garden gnome. It had expected me to be there, guarding Ben. And when the kid had needed me, I'd been passed-out drunk. Did I have any goodness within me?

The dragon roared above, impatient. It was waiting for something, certainly not its own death. Me. It waited for me. It accepted who I was without question or judgement.

"*You* created the dragon. You cut me in half," I said, my voice little more than a rasp. "That's on you."

If I embraced it, we would merge. I would become whole. The magic of this moment that Arthus had called on was there for the taking. I would return to my full self, to my full power. The dragon might hold my missing memories, or at least enough to make sense of it all. There was no surety, but it was a seductive promise. I'd spent thirty years with my life on hold. An endless procession of shit jobs and bad bosses. Every day, I'd barely scraped by, alienated from those around me, my existence only softened by a parentless kid across the street. I had paid for my crimes, hadn't I?

The lion abandoned his position by the stairs, advancing until he was just out of reach. Pain blossomed at the back of my right thigh. I twisted.

Ben held the dagger, and my blood dripped from it. Echoing tears flowed down his red and puffy cheeks, and his usually smooth features were twisted with misery. He'd found a gap in my armor and used it ruthlessly.

"I thought you were nice," he said, his eyes red, his features twisted with betrayal. "I remember it now. You used to play with me. We'd race through the castle and swim in the river. You taught me how to hold a sword, and you'd tell me tales of your battles with the ogres and the redcaps. And you had wings like your mother. You promised me you'd carry me when you learned to fly, but you never did, and I forgave you. And then you killed them. You killed my parents."

"That's right," Arthus said with a haughty laugh. "He destroyed everything you cared for and the realm your parents prized above all else. You've had your revenge, a noble act. Another awaits. I'm sorry, Your Majesty, the only way to end this once and for all is for you to sacrifice yourself. Be what the kingdom needs. A king must do no less, even if he isn't crowned."

His words slid off me, as I dropped to one knee, my leg wet with blood.

You had wings like your mother.

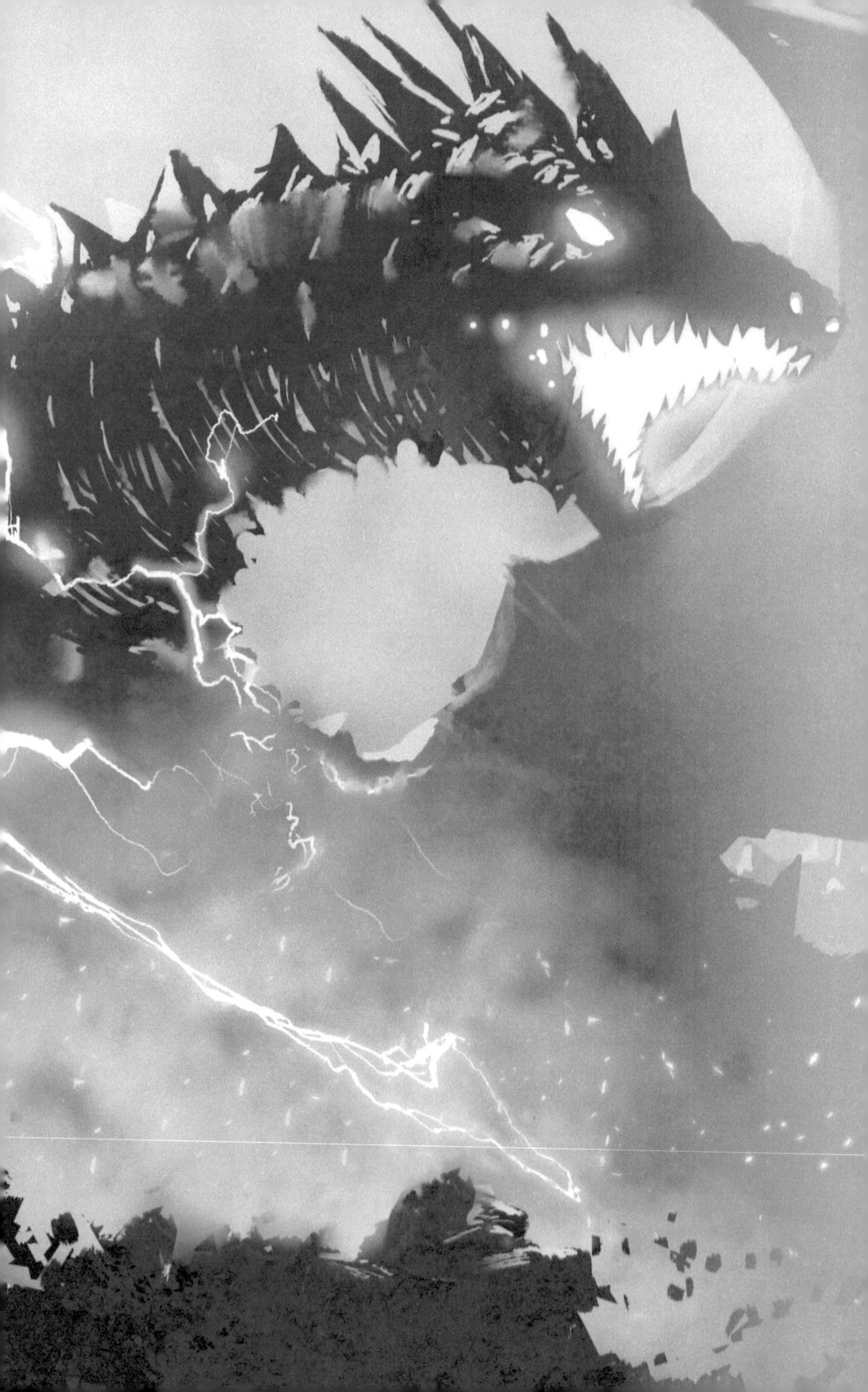

CHAPTER 8
SACRIFICE

I squeezed my eyes shut and searched for my mother, holding the concept of wings as a talisman. Wings. Golden wings. A lithe form brimming with laughter, quick to temper. Sister to the queen, elf blood mixed with that of eagles. She'd been different from the king and queen, wilder, less set in her ways. I remembered. She'd—

My body shook with loss, then with rage. "Ben, your parents ordered her death."

His grip tightened around the dagger. "Her?"

"My mother." The wolves had been on my side. This wasn't all about a dragon. There was more, much more.

Arthus kicked my good leg, and I dropped to my hands. By the time I rolled painfully onto my ass, the lion had retaken the dagger and rested a heavy paw on the boy's shoulder.

"His mother was a traitor, my prince. She had been raising an army in secret, ready to take the throne for herself. Your parents had no choice. But you do. It is time to fulfill your destiny. Just as it's time for this scum to fulfill his."

He grabbed my arm and dragged me toward the edge of the

tower. I was weak in both body and mind, but the roughness of the stone I thudded along shook free more of who I had been.

Arthus had given *it* away. I had overheard him talking to a servant. My mother had been gone for a year. Scouts had traversed the lands, searching for her—so I believed. That day, he'd spoken of a secret trial as if wracked with guilt for the cruel necessity. Seven days it had taken me to accept it as true. She couldn't be found because she was dead and burned.

She'd always quarreled with the king, once telling me he was arrogant and unbending. The conflict had grown and grown. But a traitor? I had been so sure they were wrong. And in the end, it hadn't mattered. They had to pay. Thirty days and nights I'd schemed until I could sneak into their bedchamber. I'd cut the king down, and the queen had thrown herself at me, on my sword.

I'd fled to the forest after the deed, and that's where I'd met the resistance. My life of comfort had blinded me to the suffering of the average folk, but not my mother. She hadn't been a traitor to them. I took charge of this motley cohort, still full of fury. I didn't act for their cause. It was all for me. I'd hungered to crush every vestige of those who had hurt me, though I clothed my actions with words of injustice and revolution. We'd laid siege to the castle, but we hadn't reduced it to its current state.

"Behold, dragon," Arthus bellowed while dangling me half over the edge.

Wind whipped at my hair, and I contemplated slamming onto the broken stones below.

Arthus shook me like a doll. "Dragon, if you do not land, I will kill him."

I could sense the rage that consumed the beast. My rage. And yet it beat its wings and settled nearby, energy crackling around its form like supercharged static. The tips of its golden claws were stained red. Its tail flicked back and forth, the end broad with spread feathers. The huge head jerked up and down, sizing Arthus up for a bite. It would only need one.

"Good. Now, Benedict, make your parents proud. Honor their memory. Everything rests on you. Every single life. Are you worthy, or are you selfish like your cousin?"

The boy stared at the dagger in his hand. "What do I do?"

I didn't hear the response. The dragon was stalking closer, our essences mingling at the edges. It held my rage, and I held its purpose. Arthus had filled my dragon half with magic when he'd cut it out and given it form. Reunited, we would be unstoppable. And I might be a half-blood, but I was royalty. The throne was mine for the taking. *I* would be the one to bring peace. The path to this future was simple. Arthus had to die. I reveled in the thought. And Ben. Loose ends needed trimming. The price of admission.

The dragon rose on its haunches, stealing Arthus's attention. The lion chuckled, then let go of me. Everything seemed to happen at once. He shifted his stance to pounce on Ben. I dropped, the wind in my ears and every detail of the rocks beneath standing out in excruciating detail, but I was ready for this. I grabbed hold of Arthus's leg, anchoring him and saving myself. I had my left leg up over the edge of the tower when his claws sliced across my face, drawing lines of red that burned. I screamed. He lashed out at my arm, trying to break my grip, but my armor held, and the precious seconds allowed me to scramble wholly onto the tower.

The dragon breathed fire. The blast spread quickly, the heat slamming into me as if I'd jumped into the exhaust of a jet engine. However, the beast's aim was off. Only the edge caught Arthus, burning away half his mane in an instant and leaving blackened, smoking skin and the stink of a badly cooked barbecue.

He stumbled back. "No! I am owed this."

Owed? He had torn me apart. I'd give the crispy bastard some of what he was owed. I threw myself at him, not caring how much I tore open my leg wound. He swung wildly with his clawed hands. I'd lost my sword at some point, so I ducked. He overbalanced, and I pushed.

Arthus wobbled on the tower's precipice, arms windmilling. "This can't be."

"Hell, yeah, it can," I answered. "Say hi to the king and queen for me."

I swung, pounding my fist into the unburned side of his face, upsetting his precarious balance.

He tumbled over the edge, claws reaching as he cried, "No, no! I'm meant to be king."

I watched him splatter on the rocks, a scowl forming on my brow as a harsh satisfaction gave way to confusion. What had he meant?

Events locked into order. My jaw dropped.

He'd wanted me to overhear what he'd said to the servant. He'd used me to kill the king and queen. Damn, the conniving asshole. A terrible thought occurred to me. What if he'd also used them to murder my mother in the first place, to remove a branch of the royal family? With all of us dead, there would be no obvious line of succession. He'd wanted to claim the throne for himself. He'd set me up to take the fall, but it hadn't gone to plan. I'd escaped and sent an army against him. When he got his claws on me, he screwed it up again. He'd never intended to make the dragon. He'd been torturing me, paying me back for the resistance.

I laughed, my head faint, my thoughts incredulous, as I took in the sheer bastardry. He'd planned it, sacrificed all of us on the altar of his ambition. I considered the burning city. Had he let the dragon run rampant over the land to keep the peasants busy, not counting on their desperation? Or perhaps it wasn't so calculated. He might have been barely hanging on for thirty years, for the chance to kill both dragon and prince, to cement his place as ruler. It didn't matter which. I snarled. If he'd become king, was there anything left to rule? What was the point of being at the top if all you sat on were ashes?

Fire blasted across the tower, reminding me that it wasn't over. The dragon still hunted Ben. All it saw was a threat. I stepped closer to call it off—we'd all been played—but my bad leg trembled. The blue-armored limb was awash in red. Maybe the prince had nicked an artery. I was fucked—there were no ambulances or airlifts in damn fairyland.

The sun poked above the horizon, a small hill of gold. I stumbled to my sword and picked it up. There was a chance to fix things. It all depended on what result I wanted.

"Ben, you still out there?"

The dragon craned its neck and breathed another torrent of fire. I leaned against a slab to protect myself from the wash, though it wasn't directed at me. My foot nudged a chain mail armored skeleton. A shield lay to one side. There were more dead, my mind making sense of their parts. When Arthus had cut the dragon from me, it had wreaked carnage and destruction. These were the remains of Arthus's soldiers. They'd held me down to be mutilated and paid the price.

"I'm here, Julian. You won't kill me. I was always better at hide and seek."

"I don't want to hurt you. It was all Arthus."

"You're lying. You killed my parents."

I sucked in a breath and shuffled closer to his voice. "I did. They killed my mother, and I killed them in turn. But it was Arthus pulling the strings. And even if it wasn't, they're all dead. What's the point in either of us dying now?"

It all sounded so reasonable. This wasn't going to end

without death, but elf bodies matured slowly, and so did their minds.

"I don't trust you."

The dragon roared as it climbed over the tower's crumbled stones. It couldn't find Ben, yet.

"Look, I'm going to put my sword down. I'm already bleeding out. I'm no threat to you. We need to end this. I'll call the dragon off."

Shadows stretched as sunlight bathed the tower. The dawn was slipping into day. There was a minute left, at most, and then the magic would fade forever.

"Dragon," I called out. "Heed me. Leave the boy."

The beast turned its huge head toward me. Anger radiated from its form, almost physical. It could sense my turmoil, my indecision. It didn't understand.

"Let the boy come to me."

Tilting its head back, the dragon spewed fire into the heavens.

"Ben, the dragon will find you. It's only a matter of time. I don't want that. You don't want that. I'm not going to sacrifice you like Arthus wanted to. I swear it on the grace of my mother."

Small pebbles crumbled, and Ben crawled out from a gap I would have thought too small. No wonder he'd always been able to hide so well. The dagger remained in his tight grip, the end red with my blood.

The dragon closed, its body undulating, and its wings outspread. Its head lowered toward me, and I saw myself mirrored in its eyes. We had been a being of power, the mix of elf and eagle and human, quickening, growing into something new. Some had looked at us with fear. I saw the anger in its eyes that had been my own, that and an intoxicating self-assurance. We were born to rule.

All I had to do was embrace the feathered head and let the last of the dawn magic weld us back together. When we were recombined, my wound would be as nothing. I would live. Touch wasn't enough, I admitted. It would take more. The wolf mother had said it: every magic needed its sacrifice. I finally understood what must happen.

I gazed at Ben and the dagger in his hand. "Look, kid. I put my sword down. Why don't you do the same with the dagger? We're practically brothers. You can trust me. Neither of us ever wanted this."

He stepped closer.

"That's right," I said. "There's a lot of work to be done, an entire kingdom to be rebuilt. Its folk must be brought together. Let us make a start."

I offered my hand. Ben hesitated, then stood before me. "I guess so. What—what do we do?"

"The dagger," I prompted.

He held it over my hand, clearly building the courage to let go.

The dragon roared, a bass mix of fury and disbelief. It'd sensed something through our connection. I grabbed for the dagger as the dragon launched its head forward. With a split second to choose, I pushed Ben, and the dagger spun away.

The effort sent me backward, and the dragon's maw closed on empty air. Its bestial eyes locked on me, pure hatred pinning me in place.

"Liar! Traitor!" Ben shouted as he dodged away.

"No," I called back. "The dragon's anger can't be tamed, and its thirst for power can't be quenched. If I merged back together, it would turn me into a monster. Maybe I was always destined to be one, but I don't want that. I won't let it happen. Get out of here. This is for me to do. I have to slay my own dragon. I am the sacrifice that's needed. You have to survive. This realm needs you."

Grimacing, I dropped and scooped up a long-discarded shield. The dragon breathed fire, as I knew he would. The shield caught it, sapphire flames spraying in all directions, the wood crackling, heating so fast, I could barely let go before it branded my flesh.

I leaned toward the fallen dagger, but the dragon snapped at me, and I had to spin behind stone. My sword was within reach. I picked it up, then waited, completely vulnerable as the world spun. I'd lost too much blood. It would only get worse. I felt for the buckles at the side of my breastplate, wincing, my fingers fumbling.

"So, dragon. Did I ever tell you how much of a dick we were? It was me as much as you. I let you off leash way too often."

The beast roared, its form looming over me, stealing the sunlight. If it ate me now, would we merge?

Oh, shit. That would do it.

My breastplate dropped to the ground with a clang.

"There we go." I flipped my sword and put the tip against my stomach. Uncertainty crushed my soul, but the cycle of retribution had to end. "This is where we say goodbye."

The dragon swiped, a long talon knocking the sword into the air and off the tower.

"Ah, fuck," I muttered.

That was it. I'd failed. I was a failure. I was poison. This world would have been better off if I had never been born.

The dragon roared its victory and stretched its jaws, ready to swallow me. I forced my eyes open. Those teeth would tear me to shreds. There was no question which personality would dominate, either. I'd failed, but I wasn't going to hide from my fate. It was an empty gesture, but I owed it to all those I'd hurt.

"Julian, catch!"

Silver metal swished through the air. I caught the dagger. Ben nodded, a mark of respect or forgiveness—I couldn't tell, and I didn't have time to think on it. Instead, I thrust the dagger into my flesh, feeling it bite deep.

I gasped, my innards on fire, every slight movement fresh agony. Golden smoke coiled out of the wound, magic thick in its whisps. I panted, tears streaking my cheeks. I wanted my mother to cuddle me and tell me it would be all right.

The dragon roared, sensing its chance slipping away. It hissed, then threw itself at me, teeth searching. I dove and rolled beneath it. Then, after pulling the dagger out of my flesh, I thrust it into the dragon's belly. The beast screamed, tearing the wound wider as it rocked, and I pushed the dagger deeper, right into its heart.

"Let my sacrifice bring on a thousand years of peace," I wished, crawling from beneath it with the last of my energy.

The dragon stiffened, then collapsed, so much dead meat. I went down by its side, my death racing toward me.

Ben crouched by my side.

"Peace?" I asked

He held my hand. "Peace."

I closed my eyes.

CHAPTER 9
RULE

A cacophony of thuds and cries battered my skull. There must be an afterlife. I knew where I belonged. I opened my eyes, ready for my fate. I was inside a white tent, lying on a cot. That was odd. I was expecting more of a fire and brimstone motif. I tried to rise, and every inch of my body screeched with pain, silent klaxons that couldn't be ignored. Giving in, I stared upward, panting.

"So, you're awake." A fuzzy face looked down at me. I knew it. It was the rabbit I'd freed, Jessica Lightfoot. "I better tell him."

Before I could ask a question, she bounded out of the tent. Where was I? What had happened? I couldn't wait. I pressed my teeth together and grunted, forcing my abused body to comply. First shifting into a sitting position, then standing, wavering like wheat in a breeze. I stumbled to the end of the tent, leaned on a pole, and pushed my way out.

There were many other tents, each by the castle wall on a shelf of mostly flat ground. All around bipedal animals worked, clearing debris, shoring up leaning walls, and a myriad of other tasks I couldn't discern. From my vantage, I could see the city.

The smoke had gone, leaving charred remains. Not all of the city had burned, and I thought I could see movement.

Closer by, I heard talking and laughter, genuine happiness, the sort tinged with sadness that made it all the more beautiful. When had I last heard that? The kingdom was alive. Arthus and I—and perhaps others—had poured our poison into its heart for our selfish wants, and yet, here it was, healing. My eyes grew moist. I stood there, taking it all in, embracing the joy of those who worked for a common good, as if there was a chance some could soak into me.

"He's over here," Jessica's voice said from out of sight.

Ben came from behind the tents, dressed in well-made but practical clothing, a yellow tunic, a red overshirt, navy pants, polished black boots. His right arm was in a green sling. The colors were garish, but I remembered it was the way of this world. A wolf and a sheep followed behind, each armored, each with serious expressions.

"How are you feeling?"

"Feeling like I'm not dead. Which is good, I guess, though it hurts more. I don't understand."

Ben lifted his arm out of the sling. It was bandaged and oddly short, the end a stump. My skin turned clammy. I'd failed him even when sacrificing myself. He couldn't wield a sword. A thousand years of peace? He'd always be under threat.

"I—I'm sorry." I croaked. It wasn't enough. Nothing could be. Yes, he'd lived for many decades, but he was still a kid. It wasn't enough, but I said it again. "I'm sorry."

"Cousin, don't be. You sacrificed yourself for me—for everyone—and I had to make a sacrifice to save you. There was just enough magic left to perform the healing," he said, placing his arm back in the sling. "Arthus taught me a little of his knowledge when I was younger, before—" His voice trailed off.

Others gathered around, a sea of fur and feathers and scales.

The sound of work had stopped. Their faces were expectant, but I had no idea what they were waiting to see.

He walked to me and clasped my forearm with his remaining hand. There was a dignity beneath his youthful features. He was a child by elf standards, but he'd still lived many years.

"You gave up everything to save me—the throne, unmatched power, and your life. But that's not why I mutilated myself. I did this because you came for me when you didn't know who I was. It took me a while to understand. That's who you *really* are. You didn't have to, but you did. You're a good man. And now, you need to be a good king."

I shook my head. "King?"

"I am damaged. We are cousins. The blood of my line also runs through you. We need a strong leader, one who won't look from the top of a castle and see ants to be toyed with. You gave up power. You risked yourselves over and over for those you barely knew. You will rule well."

I leaned back against the tent, horror tightening the skin on my face. "No. I won't. That's a terrible idea." I might have slayed my dragon, but I didn't want to be tempted. I couldn't risk it. The answer came to me and I put a hand on his. "I won't be king. You will, but if you'll have me, I'll be your right hand."

Shaking, I dropped to one knee. "Your majesty, will you accept my service?"

He tilted his head, then looked around. The animals lowered themselves, heads bowed.

"I guess I'm king then." He looked every bit as young as I had once thought him to be.

"Don't worry," I said. "I'll still chase you around the castle. And we can teach this lot to play soccer."

He laughed, and the crowd cheered. The cycle was broken.

I didn't know when I'd see Earth again. I didn't know if I

would. But I had purpose and something I hadn't known I'd been missing for thirty years—I had family. And peace, or at least the promise of it.

I took a shuddering breath and felt the weight of all that had passed. "But first, my king, I need to rest."

He grinned. "Already starting with the demands? I guess I can allow that. But don't take too long. I need you. We all do."

About the Author

Robert writes gripping science fiction, urban fantasy, and epic fantasy for adults and children. When he's not writing, he's swinging swords for fun and bruises. He has also written works for adults and children under the name R Max Tillsley.

You can find him at:

https://www.tillsley.com

and:

facebook.com/rmaxtillsley

instagram.com/rmaxtillsley

bsky.app/profile/tillsley.bsky.social

bookbub.com/authors/robert-tillsley